THE DRESSING-UP DAD

To Mark Wallington, who once dressed up as a turtle. MS
For Sam, James and Bea. PH

OXFORD
UNIVERSITY PRESS

Great Clarendon Street, Oxford OX2 6DP
Oxford University Press is a department of the University of Oxford.
It furthers the University's objective of excellence in research, scholarship,
and education by publishing worldwide. Oxford is a registered trade mark of
Oxford University Press in the UK and in certain other countries

Text copyright © Maudie Smith 2017
Illustrations copyright © Paul Howard 2017

The moral rights of the author and illustrator have been asserted
Database right Oxford University Press (maker)

First published 2017

British Library Cataloguing in Publication Data

Data available

ISBN: 978-0-19-274979-6 (paperback)
ISBN: 978-0-19-275871-2 (eBook)

1 3 5 7 9 10 8 6 4 2

Printed in China

Paper used in the production of this book is a natural,
recyclable product made from wood grown in sustainable forests.
The manufacturing process conforms to the environmental
regulations of the country of origin.

THE DRESSING-UP DAD

MAUDIE SMITH

PAUL HOWARD

OXFORD
UNIVERSITY PRESS

Danny **loved**
dressing up.

So did Danny's dad!

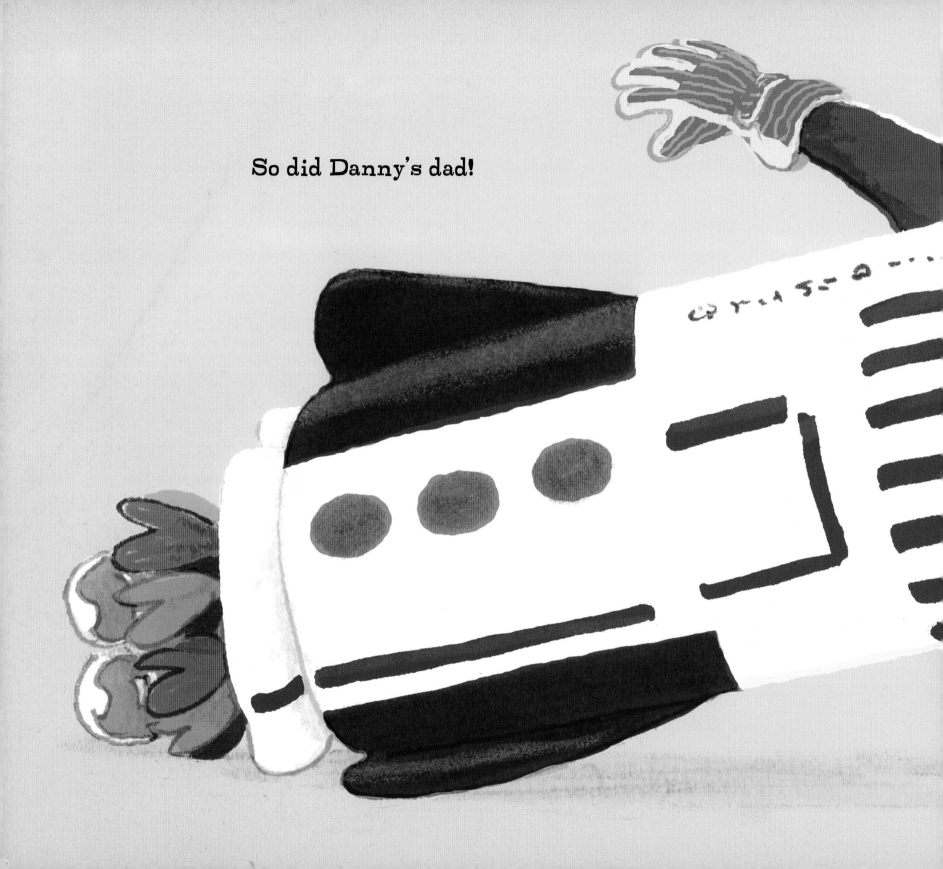

Danny and his Dad dressed up at home . . .

. . . and when they went out!

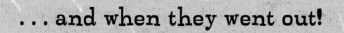

They dressed up anywhere,

at any time . . .

. . . whatever the weather.

And there was nothing they enjoyed more . . .

... than a dressing-up party!

For his birthday Danny had a **dinosaur party.**

The next year he had a **robot party.**

And the year after that it was **pirates**.

Dad was the most piratey pirate of them all!

There was no one quite like Danny's Dad . . .

But sometimes
Danny wondered.

He wondered what it would be like to have
an ordinary everyday dad . . .

. . . like other people had.

'Your birthday's coming up,' said Danny's dad. 'I'm really looking forward to the bugs party . . .

. . . what shall I come as?

A ladybird?

A dragon fly?

Or a
great big
hairy spider?'

Danny ran upstairs.

'I don't want you to come to my party as a bug,' he said.

'Not even as a beetle?' said Dad.

'Not even as an ant! Can't you come as a dad instead? An ordinary everyday one. Please?'

'Oh,' said Dad.

'I could try being
an ordinary everyday
dad. Although I'm not
sure I have the
right outfit.'

But at the very
back of the wardrobe,
Danny found the
perfect thing.

Danny's dad looked great dressed up as an ordinary everyday dad.

He turned out to be really good at **being** an ordinary everyday dad too.

He took care of the guests.

He organised the
party games.

And he made sure everyone
got a slice of birthday cake.

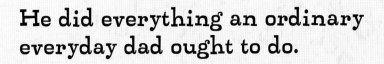

He did everything an ordinary
everyday dad ought to do.

But something wasn't right.

'We want to be chased,' said Danny's friends.
'We want a giant caterpillar!'

Dad looked sad. 'Sorry,' he said.
'I've got party bags to organise.'

But Danny shouted, 'WAIT! Put it on, Dad. Go ahead.'

'I'd love to,' said Dad.
  'But are you sure you want me to?'

'Quite sure,' said Danny.
  It was his party but he wanted
  Dad to have fun too.

So Dad dressed up as a giant caterpillar . . .

And it was brilliant!

No one wanted to go home.

'You love dressing up, don't you, Dad?' said Danny.

'I do,' said Dad. 'I love dressing up with you.'

'Well, from now on,' said Danny, 'we can dress up together whenever you like.'

Ordinary everyday dads were fine . . .

. . . but Danny knew his dressing-up dad

was the best dad in the world!

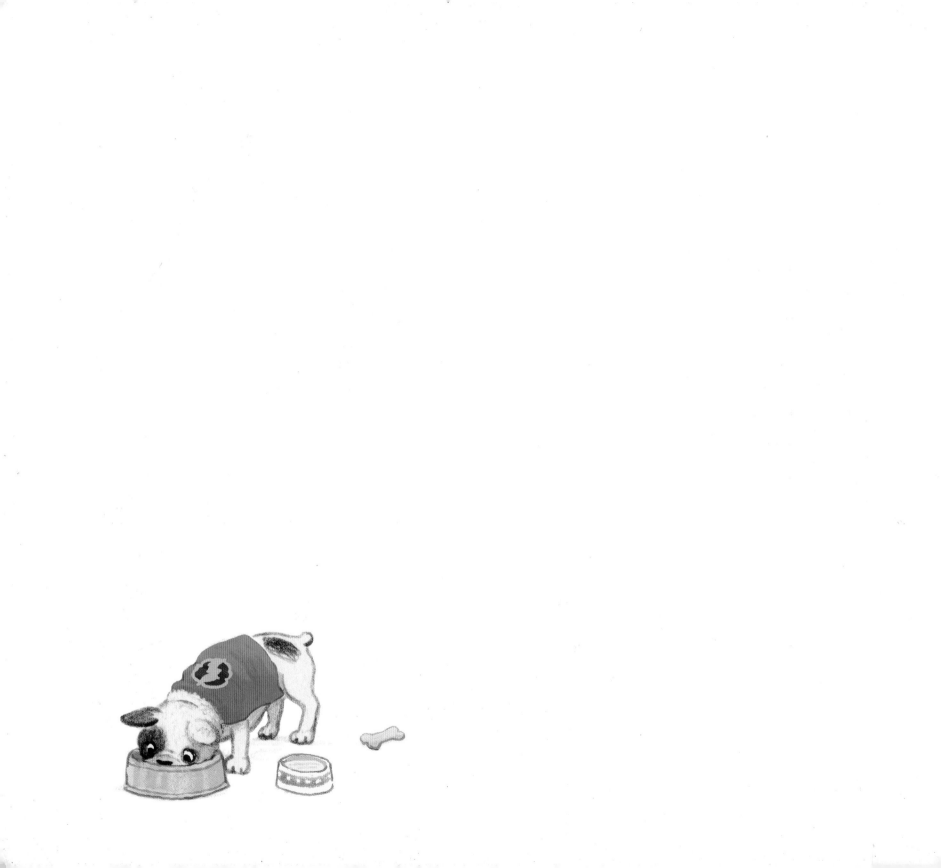